SERENDIPITY

TOBI TOBIAS

Serendipity

ILLUSTRATED BY

PETER H. REYNOLDS

SIMON & SCHUSTER BOOKS FOR YOUNG READERS

NEW YORK   LONDON   TORONTO   SYDNEY   SINGAPORE

SIMON & SCHUSTER BOOKS FOR YOUNG READERS
An imprint of Simon & Schuster Children's Publishing Division
1230 Avenue of the Americas, New York, New York 10020

Book design by Heather Wood
The text of this book is set in Berliner Grotesk Light.
The illustrations are rendered in watercolor and ink.
Printed in Hong Kong
2 4 6 8 10 9 7 5 3 1

Library of Congress Cataloging-in-Publication Data
Tobias, Tobi.
Serendipity / Tobi Tobias ; illustrated by Peter H. Reynolds.–1st ed.
p.   cm.
Summary : A child ponders the pleasant results of serendipity, such as getting extra pieces from the gumball machine,
having a peanut in your pocket when you meet a squirrel, or finding a five-dollar bill.
ISBN 0-689-83373-3
[1. Serendipity–Fiction. 2. Chance–Fiction. 3. Luck–Fiction.] I. Reynolds, Peter, ill. II Title.
PZ7.T56 Se 2000   [E]–dc21   99-086469

For Will and Jim,
princes of serendipity

−T.T.

For my twin, Paul.
Serendipity is being born
then discovering you have a twin!

−P.H.R.

SERENDIPITY

is putting a quarter
in the gumball machine
and having three pieces
come rattling out
instead of one—

all red.

SERENDIPITY is getting to the zoo

just when it's feeding time for the seals.

SERENDIPITY is blowing out all your birthday candles in one breath—

and having your wish come true.

SERENDIPITY is when
you spill *another* glass of milk,
and your mom says,
"Accidents will happen."

$\mathcal{S}$ E R E N D I P I T Y is a hole
in the sweater you always hated.

SERENDIPITY is meeting a squirrel—

and having a peanut in your pocket.

Or finding a five-dollar bill when you're helping Grampa clear out his garage,

and Grampa saying, "It's yours."

$\text{\textbf{S}}$ E R E N D I P I T Y is when your big sister and her friends
are giggling over some secret,

and it turns out to be a surprise for *you*.

S E R E N D I P I T Y is when your old stuffed bear—that you really don't care about anymore, except you used to sleep with it—

isn't lost.

SERENDIPITY is when you have to go
to your grouchy Aunt Bea's house,

and–guess what!–
her dog, Banjo, just had puppies.

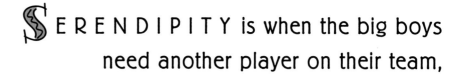

SERENDIPITY is when the big boys
need another player on their team,

and you happen to be carrying your glove.

S E R E N D I P I T Y is when you find out
you actually look *better* in glasses.

S E R E N D I P I T Y is snow during winter vacation,

no rain on the Fourth of July.

SERENDIPITY
is seeing a rainbow.

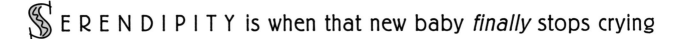
SE R E N D I P I T Y is when that new baby *finally* stops crying

and then laughs only for you.

SERENDIPITY is when your mom and dad say,
"There's so much work to do around this house,

we might as well all go to the movies."

SERENDIPITY
is meeting someone

who's going to be
your best friend forever.

SERENDIPITY is a word that,
when you find out what it means,

is as wonderful and surprising as it sounds.